STORMWORLD

Stormworld

Brian Herbert & Bruce Taylor

WordFire Press
Colorado Springs, Colorado

Published by
WordFire Press, an imprint of
WordFire Inc
PO Box 1840
Monument CO 80132

ISBN: 978-1-61475-051-2

WordFire Press Trade Paperback Edition: January 2013
Printed in the USA

www.wordfire.com

Contents

Dedication

This book is dedicated to Janet Herbert and Roberta Gregory,
for your creative, intelligent suggestions,
and your loving support.

Acknowledgments

The authors wish to thank the following individuals for reviewing the background science in this story: Richard Gammon, Professor Emeritus of Chemistry and Oceanography, University of Washington; and Patrick Mazza, Research Director for Climate Solutions.

For manuscript critiques, the authors would like to thank Joel Davis, Roberta Gregory, Janet Herbert, Patricia MacEwan, Linda Shepherd, and Faith Szafranski.

Preface

In a sudden and shocking die-off of humanity, only five percent of the world population remained. Bodies piled up so quickly that they were usually left to the elements for disposal. Among the clusters of survivors, new and often violent social groups formed. London, Paris, New York, Seattle, and other major cities became burned-out ghost towns, ruled by roving bands of brigands. These armed gangs even terrorized impoverished people in the countryside, who were barely surviving on decimated food resources.

All over the world, religious fanatics bred. Every major religion became dominated by a radical belief system, as the remaining population sought explanation and solace for what had happened. Few knew how to cope with the horrific events occurring all around them, and suicide was, by far, at the highest level in history.

In America and other western nations, fanatical Christians pointed to end-of-the-world predictions made in the *Book of Revelations* of the *Bible*. Numerous religious cults formed enclaves in remote locations to survive the ongoing cataclysm, and to await the Second Coming of Jesus and the Rapture.

It was as if every human killing element on the planet had been unleashed at once—even worse than the ten plagues of ancient Egypt. Immense disasters affected the land, the sky, and the water, causing starvation and pandemic outbreaks of disease. There were floods, earthquakes, ferocious winds, and war, on a scale never known before.

In the aftermath, a sickly, smoky sky covered most of the world, blocking the sun. On those rare occasions when the sun came out, people stared at it in awe, sometimes blinding themselves in the brilliance, as if thinking it was the light of God, signifying their rescue. But no salvation was imminent, only dismal, squalid times, growing worse by the hour. All of Earth had become what used to be known as the "third world"....

As our story begins, only ragtag remnants of legitimate governmental agencies remain, and militias are poorly armed. Overseeing it all from the remains of the United States is Conelrad, a fledging government of international scientists that is trying to make decisions for the welfare of the entire planet, and not for particular regions. But these valiant men and women are essentially powerless, representing the withering hope that some sense of normalcy might return one day. The improvised government has very little real influence, and only limited paramilitary capabilities.

Chapter 1

A Promise of Protection

Abe Tojiko's stomach growled. Still hungry. Always hungry. Looking in the mirror this morning, he saw the taut, stretched skin, the sunken brown eyes and prematurely gray hair. Had he ever really been overweight? He had lost nearly a hundred pounds on his six-foot-one frame, and barely weighed 150 pounds. From constant stress and lack of sleep, shadows had set in beneath his glowering, haunted eyes. Only thirty-eight, he felt twice that age.

With a deep sigh he tried to put the depressing thoughts aside, and went downstairs to check the seed storage chambers, where he monitored the critical humidity and temperature settings. So far, the electrical problems they'd been having had only affected some of the interior doors—God help them if the exterior blast door was ever breached by intruders, or if the seed vault temperatures varied from where they were supposed to be.

Soon his thoughts drifted off. He had worked there so long that he could hardly remember his prior life, which seemed like a distant, halcyon time, a fleeting dream. His pretty wife, three children, his parents, a brother, a sister ... how long had it been since he'd seen them, just before they were all killed? Three, or was it four years?

Halcyon was a comparative word. There had been severe climatic fluctuations in those bygone days with his family, causing Abe to move them to higher ground to avoid the immense coastal and river floods that wiped out cities, towns, and crops, relegating entire landscapes to oblivion. He had used his scientific knowledge to select a region where the winds were not expected to reach the dangerous velocities that had been seen in many regions of the world. He selected Beaumont in northeastern Wyoming, a small town at an elevation of 4400 feet, sheltered from the prevailing winds by a mountain range. All available information told him it would be safe there.

After assuring himself that they were all secure in their new lives, Abe returned to his job at the seed bank in Washington state. But a month later, a storm with winds exceeding 350 miles per hour hit northeast Wyoming, scouring the land, turning the once-pristine region into a hellish, lifeless blast zone. Afterward, Abe had only one family, his fellow employees in the Cascade Seed Repository — a facility that was built into blasted-out mountain bedrock.

Now through thick glass walls on the lowest level of the facility, he saw two men and a tall, blonde woman in adjacent chambers, monitoring the precious treasure house that contained every key plant seed in the world, along with a broad selection of tubers, roots, and bulbs. With this raw material, they could recreate everything from desert palms to tundra grasses, and even a number of flowers that served no purpose beyond their physical beauty.

The blonde glanced at Abe, but she did not smile. They were not lovers anymore. Belinda Amar had gone on to Jimmy Hansik, a former body-builder who performed general maintenance, but who had made a number of serious mistakes, causing valuable seeds to be endangered. He should have been fired or reassigned, but had a charming way of convincing Director Jackson that the problems were not his fault. A total of six employees lived and worked in the huge, bunker-like facility, and they didn't always get along.

Employees.

Abe mused over the word, as he made an entry in a hand-held datacube. Like "halcyon" and "family," the word didn't mean what it used to. Most of the time, he felt more like a prisoner than an employee.

Immense environmental disasters had a way of destroying not only habitats, but also the old ways of thinking and saying things. Inside the bombproof, stormproof seed storage facility no worker had received a paycheck for more than ten months, but everyone kept going anyway, surviving and adapting, trying to forget what they had lost.

Behind Abe, an interior door opened, but made an odd, squealing noise that Jimmy had not diagnosed yet. Abe felt a sensation of pressure change. The stocky, dark-skinned Director of Operations stomped in, a perpetual frown on his gray-bearded face. He wore a white laboratory smock with chemical stains on it. "New message from Con," he said, waving a printout in the air.

Benitar Jackson was referring to Conelrad, what the remnants of the United Sates government called itself, after the name of America's first emergency broadcasting system. It was an acronym for Control of Electromagnetic Radiation. The federal government, which once employed millions of people, was only a shadow of its former self. In its place, a skeleton administration of scientists operated from a mountainside bunker in Maryland, sending out queries and orders via a satellite communications system that hung on by only the barest technological threads. Of the satellites in orbit, some of the crucial ones were non-operating, for lack of shuttle repairs. The communications were getting spottier and spottier. Many messages did not get through at all.

Abe read the dispatch. It was brief but urgent:

Cascade Seed Repository:

You are now the last undamaged seed bank in the world. We intend to send a military force to protect you, but circumstances make it impossible to promise a date. In the meantime, notify all personnel to arm themselves and remain on the highest state of alert. Keep in mind that weather-tracking data (and all other information) will be intermittent due to ongoing technical problems. As for the electrical problems you cited, we have no suggestions. You will have to figure them out on-site, giving priority to seed vault temperatures.

—Conelrad HQ

"Guess we have job security now," Abe said. "Say, isn't it about time you distributed those firearms you've been hoarding?"

Jackson's bright green eyes flashed. "I'll decide when the time is proper!" He snatched the printout from Abe and stalked off.

The Director, whom Abe referred to as "Top Seed," had not smiled for a long time, and Abe worried about the older man's mental and physical health. Even faced with the tyranny of the Director, Abe always tried to see the good in him, the way he'd dedicated his life to such an important cause. As for Abe, even through the most difficult of times he cultivated his own sense of humor, as if tending to a precious plant. He found laughter therapeutic, enabling him to get through problems.

Entering the chamber through a thick glass door, Belinda grimaced and asked, "Couldn't you show him just a little more respect?"

"I was just kidding him. He knows I respect him."

The tall blonde scowled. "Be careful. If you go too far he could just eliminate you and build a robot to take your place. I've seen him tinkering in his workshop late at night."

"Yeah, well if he did that, he'd miss me. I provide a lot of the entertainment around here … not only for him, but for the others. I'm the voice of sanity, keeping people on their toes, and he knows it, no matter what he says."

"Benitar is nuts, you know," she said. "and smart, with that personal escape capsule he has for himself, kept where the rest of us can't get to it."

"I'd rather call him focused than nuts," Abe said. But there were troubling aspects of the Director's personality, he admitted to himself, including things he didn't bother to explain to any of the staff. Before the weather went into the deep freeze, the wealthy Jackson had designed and built a rocket-propelled capsule, which he had fitted into a chamber on the upper level, donating his own funds to the government for this, and supposedly getting their approval. Calling it the "emergency seed-evacuation capsule," Benitar said he had a sampling of seeds stored on board, and that the rest of the craft was only big enough for one person. None of the staff had ever been permitted to see the vessel, nor did they know the access and launch codes.

"It gives me an uneasy feeling just knowing it's up there," Belinda said, looking upward, "while the rest of us poor saps don't have anything like it."

He looked at her intently, and changed the subject, since matters involving Benitar were often pointless and frustrating to discuss, because no one could do anything about them. "I hear you went topside this morning," Abe said. "What's the weather like out there?"

"White on the ground, gray in the sky."

"Same as usual."

She shook her head. "Deeper snow and a darker, lower cloud cover. Wind is whipping up. Looks like we're in for another blizzard — Who knows? Maybe the mother of them all."

Chapter 2

Dumped Into the Devil Zone

The young woman carried a backpack as she trudged along a snowy road that wound through a thick forest of evergreens, their boughs drooping under heavy winter loads. The road showed only animal tracks. No vehicles had passed this way in a long time. As her boots crunched through the ice and snow, Peggy Atkins wondered if she had been there previously, before the midday storm had covered her tracks. All around, she heard the eerie snapping of branches as they finally gave way under the weight of snow.

For days she had been wandering along narrow highways and logging roads, unable to get her bearings because the daytime sky was always gray, with no glimmer of sunshine. She could not think of a worse place to be, and sometimes felt herself wishing it would all be over soon, and that she could just lie down in the snow and go to sleep. She would do exactly that, too, if not for the unborn child in her womb.

Peggy shivered and gathered her coat collar tightly around her neck, re-buttoning the top snap that kept coming undone. Her blue eyes stared dully down, at her footfall. She wondered if she would ever bathe again, ever have her black hair clean and shiny, the way it used to be. How long had it been since she had even looked in a mirror at her reflection, since she had leisurely brushed her hair? The simple pleasures seemed so important to her now, and so irretrievable. Placing one foot in front of the other, she kept going, trudging along, her muscles aching for the relief she couldn't give them.

Her old life was gone, and she hardly wanted to think about it, how things had gone so horribly wrong between her and her lover, and he'd hired someone to kill her—a plot that she foiled, fleeing for her life and the life of her unborn child.

The night before, Peggy had slept inside a crude lean-to that she had fashioned from sticks and fallen cedar boughs, but when nightfall arrived in a couple of hours, she had no idea where she would find shelter, if at all. She knew only one thing, that she should not remain in one place for any longer than necessary. She had to keep looking, trying to find a way out of this hellish wilderness. The crazy men who had driven her out there and dumped her had called it the "Devil Zone," a place where sinners entered, but did not leave.

During her stay in the town, when it had still been a sanctuary for her, she'd heard of the zone, before it had become her sentence. An old man at the general store had compared it with the Bermuda Triangle, except on a smaller scale, a place where people disappeared under mysterious circumstances.

She didn't see how everything had gone so bad for her. At first, the people of the mountain town had welcomed her, taking her into their homes and inviting her to share their sparse meals with them. Soon, she began to see that they had strict religious views, but this didn't particularly alarm her. These days, a lot of religious communes had sprung up in remote regions, and she was sure that most of their members were good-hearted people.

Suspecting her situation as an unwed mother might be a problem with some of these backwoods folks, Peggy had concealed her condition at first. But as months passed and she began to show, she'd finally confided in a woman who had provided her with a room, telling her that the father had refused to marry her ... and about the money and power he had, the way he wanted her dead and had the means to accomplish it.

Within hours, the story spread through town like a sudden storm and she began to notice hard, accusatory stares from people who had been pleasant to her previously, and mutterings that soon escalated to outright condemnation. A child out of wedlock! That was all they thought about, all they focused on. No sympathy for her at all, only blame. She must have brought it on herself, they said, she must be lying about him.

At the clapboard church, the minister, a cultist who called himself "The Faithfinder," condemned her as a fallen woman and a symbol of everything that had gone wrong in the world. A wild-eyed man with a straggly beard, he held a town meeting one evening and said, "Untamed thou art in our midst, a wild and uncultured thing. Go, ye, harlot. We banish you to the Devil Zone where you can fornicate and be bestial, out of our sight."

"But—but—I—I will be lost out there and—and—" In the front row of the church, tears streamed down Peggy's face and she sobbed, "Why, why if the father refused to marry me and did all the rest—why am I considered fallen? What about him?"

"Enough," thundered The Faithfinder. "Enough of your sniveling excuses, trying to weaken our resolve and make us think you are still pure and only a victim. Enough, Daughter of Eve, for you must have enticed the man, causing him to go astray."

"No! It wasn't like that!" She rose to her feet in indignation.

"Silence!" he shouted.

"But my baby!"

"You should have thought of that months ago," the minister said.

As she sputtered protests, the minister and two deacons forced her into an off-road vehicle and blindfolded her. In the middle of the night, they drove her to a wilderness area and dumped her out into the snow beside a logging road, throwing a heavy parka, a flashlight, and a pack of supplies after her.

The Faithfinder had shouted at her, "If God wants you to survive, if thou art truly a chaste woman in heart, you will survive." He and his companions then drove off, leaving her in the forest, dimly illuminated by a rarely-seen moon, piercing through the cloud cover.

Shaking with anger and shivering in the cold, Peggy had bundled up as much as possible and put the pack on. Then, saving the flashlight battery as much as possible, she had followed the tracks of the vehicle in the snow, thinking she might find her way back out—until a sudden snowfall hit.

Chapter 3

Abe Finds Peggy

Early the following morning, Abe activated a melter to clear the exterior blast door of the seed repository. Poking his head out of the bunker-like facility, he saw an unfamiliar shape on the nearby hillside, covered in snow. Perhaps a hundred feet upslope at the edge of the forest, he made out a bump of icy whiteness with branches and fir boughs sticking out of the top. Had a tree fallen over?

As part of his normal security detail, he marched through the deep snow to investigate. Plodding up the slope, he came to the mysterious form, and catching his breath, he cleared snow away and broke into a makeshift enclosure. Inside, he saw a human figure in a dark blue parka, lying on a silver-colored thermal blanket. A woman. She wore insulated clothing, but had no sleeping bag.

She was facing toward him, her eyes closed, and he couldn't tell if she was breathing. Clearing away more branches, he crawled into the shelter. Removing one of his gloves as he knelt by her and touched the carotid artery on her neck. It pulsed.

"Miss!" he said in a loud voice, "Miss! Wake up!"

She did not respond. Concerned, Abe wondered what to do. He couldn't leave her out there, and her prospects were not good if he took her inside the seed repository. Director Jackson did not like intruders, and had already ordered the execution of four men who had ventured into the surrounding clearing and nearby forest, citing security concerns and lack of resources to house and feed strangers.

"We must protect the seeds at all costs," he had said repeatedly, as he ordered Jimmy Hansik to dump the men in the woods and leave them for animals to tear to pieces. The security of the seeds was Benitar's catchall excuse, justifying anything distasteful that he wanted to do.

Abe picked her up in his arms. She was not particularly heavy, but having lost so much of his own weight and strength, he struggled under the burden. With considerable difficulty, he carried her inside the seed repository, closing the heavy blast door behind him. Her face had turned a pale shade of blue. She seemed to be in a coma, and would have died outside anyway. Without a doubt, Jackson was going to say she should have been left outside, but Abe couldn't do it.

Dreading the trouble he would be in, he made his way along a corridor. At this early hour, no one else was up in this section. After laying the woman gently on his own bed, he went back outside and destroyed the lean-to, scattering its parts so that no sign of it remained. Then, just as the snow began to fall again, he scooped up her backpack and other personal articles, and sought shelter in the bunker.

This time Benitar Jackson awaited him at the bed, having seen the activities on a security camera. Though Abe sympathized with the Director, at times the man seemed like a textbook case of paranoia, always on the lookout for traitors on his staff, and for mobs of people he feared would come and break into the repository, stealing the seeds that were more precious to him than anything. In a world of finite resources, Jackson said that "seeds" (a catchall word that included the tubers, roots, and bulbs he stored) had become the most rare and valuable items in existence, more dear than gold, platinum, or any other of the other articles that men had always valued, throughout history. With the terrible events that had occurred all over the world, he was right about this, of course, but that didn't make it any easier to live with the man, and work with him.

"What do you think you're doing?" Jackson demanded. His hands were inside the deep pockets of his stained smock, and Abe knew he always carried a gun in one of them.

"Showing a little human concern, something you should understand."

"Our seeds are for all of humanity," Jackson snapped. "Isn't it human to preserve them?"

Ignoring him for the moment, Abe wiped melted snow off the woman and removed her jacket, gloves and boots. Everything was wet. "I'll get Belinda in here to dress her in dry clothes," he said.

"For what? Her execution?"

"You might want to rethink that," Abe said, placing a hand on her protruding belly. "Looks to me like she's pregnant." At that very moment, as if emphasizing his point, he felt something kick against his palm, a tiny fetus speaking out in the only way it knew how.

Chapter 4

Peggy Keeps a Journal

As days passed, Peggy exercised regularly, at least as much as she could, considering her condition and the spatial limitations of the facility. She developed a routine of walking rapidly through the areas of the seed bank that were not off-limits to her, a route of perhaps a quarter mile. She tried not to think of how much she felt trapped in this windowless bunker, essentially sentenced there against her will, and how claustrophobia had always been one of her biggest fears. Desperately, she wanted to leave, to get back out into the open air, but circumstances did not permit it. She had to think first of her baby's welfare, and not of her own.

Each afternoon, Peggy made entries in a journal, sheets of lined paper in a spiral ring notebook that she found in a seed-bank office and slipped into her clothing, beneath a sweater that Belinda had given to her. On her first writing foray, Peggy came up with only a few sentences, but soon found herself filling pages on both sides and flipping sheets of paper quickly as she scribbled. Using three colors of ink from different pens, depending upon her mood, she wrote in blue, green, or red. Her feelings were new to her since she had never been pregnant before, but she thought her child might like to read these entries someday. As the words flowed before her, she began to feel free to say whatever she pleased on the pages. It was an escape from confinement of sorts, and she loved the new time alone, in which she basically talked to the pages. Committing her innermost thoughts to words, she described the seed bank employees, the routines they followed, and the eccentricities of their personalities.

She always wrote in the privacy of her tiny (though unlockable) sleeping room, then hid the journal afterward behind the bed. There, low on a wall by one corner, she had found a loose metal plate that someone had used to cover an apparent construction defect, using screws that didn't hold in the concrete when she pulled at it. Behind the plate, a small, dark hole opened up that she couldn't see the end of. The precious journal fit in there easily, and she put it in a thick plastic bag in an effort to protect it from any moisture that might be in there, or rodents. Then, like a prisoner in a cell tunneling a secret escape route, she jammed a table against the plate to hold it against the wall, thus enabling her to get into and out of the compartment at will. Most of the people in the seed bank would not like what she had to say about them. Director Jackson, in particular.

I promised myself that I won't go crazy here, she wrote in one of her first entries, *but I hate this place and the people in it, even the ones who are nice to me. Some days are worse than others, as my emotions fluctuate wildly. Often I can tell how bad, or how good a day is gong to be, based upon how I feel when I get up and start to move around. I always eat breakfast in the concrete-walled employee cafeteria: imitation eggs and sausages, and other foods from cans and shrink-wrap packages—with all portions strictly controlled, because supplies are dwindling. During breakfast, I continue to gauge my mood, trying to be upbeat. But with the chemical and psychic turmoil going on inside me, that is not always possible. Whenever I feel especially anxious or depressed, I find that I can't talk with others at all, not even with Abe Tojiko, who has been so nice and helpful to me. I try not to offend anyone, and particularly the Director of Operations, Benitar Jackson. What a strange, aggressive man he is; I can hardly see the good in him that Abe points out. I've figured out Jackson's schedule and I take every effort to avoid him.*

Two weeks into her narrative, Peggy's personal observations and feelings took a backseat to events outside the seed bank and around the world. In one of her entries she wrote: *An F-5 tornado has just passed within a mile of here — Abe and I saw it on the projection screen in the weather room. Remote sensors report the base was more than half a mile across — something I would have thought impossible. Watching it on the screen gave me an unreal sensation, as if it was only a scary movie, or a bleak news report about some far off place, not Western Washington. Winds registered at 304 miles per hour! Conelrad says the main highway to Seattle is impassable, with roadways ripped up, choked with debris, and a main bridge destroyed.*

Just then she heard a noise, and looked up. Of all the sleeping quarters in the seed repository, only Director Jackson's room could locked. She had jammed a towel under her own door for privacy, to make it stick a little if anyone tried to get in, but Abe pushed it open with only a little difficulty and stepped into the room. He wore a long-sleeved blue shirt and jeans.

Quickly, she closed the binder and let it fall behind the bed.

"Oh, sorry," he said, "I knocked, but didn't hear any response. The surveillance system has been breaking down, and the Director wants to know where you are at all times. I was told to ..." The slender man scowled. "Say, what were you doing there?"

"Nothing," she said, feeling her face flush hot.

He nodded, but had seen something.

"It's just a journal," she admitted.

"You'd better hide it well," said Abe.

Peggy nodded. "Don't tell anyone, OK? You can read it if you want. Well, I'd rather you didn't, but you're the only person I trust here, and I don't want you to think I'm some kind of saboteur or spy or anything. If you have to read it, go ahead."

He grinned. "Does it say you think I'm cute?"

With a gentle smile, Peggy said, "Maybe, and maybe not. Maybe I said you're overbearing, and I can't stand you."

Abe looked hurt. "But you trust me?"

"Mostly, though you may be a bit naive when it comes to assessing Jackson. I suspect he's darker than you want to admit."

Abe nodded. "Perhaps." He paused, smiled tentatively. "It's nice to hear that you trust me, because I do care about you."

"A woman's feelings are complex, especially when she's going to have a baby."

She searched his eyes, saw kindness there.

"No, I didn't write that you're cute," she said, "though come to think of it, you are, kind of. With all the stresses we're under, I haven't had time to think about such things, and I've already had a bad relationship. Her eyes misted over. "I just want my baby safe."

"I know, Peggy, and I'm here for you if you need me. Just let me know what I can do."

"Thanks, you're a big help." She smiled shyly as she watched him back out of the room and close the door. She jammed the towel back under the door, more tightly this time.

Using green ink for no conscious reason, she continued writing in her journal, setting down information she had learned in the seed bank's weather room: *I can't believe how bizarre the weather has become. Abe and Belinda told me that catastrophes started occurring after the deep ocean current failed, causing serious climatic changes. Last week it was 137 degrees Fahrenheit in Madrid, and two days later it dropped to 21. Now it's 14 degrees in New York on August 20! The tropics are sweltering through deadly levels of heat and humidity — 142 degrees in Caracas with 99% humidity, 138 degrees in Djakarta, 136 in Kuala Lumpur. People are still dying. It's beyond comprehension.*

Abe says he used to think the Pacific Northwest was somehow immune, even after the deep ocean current failed — that for a while it wasn't that bad here, though cool — a high of 39 degrees last July 4th. Still, we weren't having the 250 mph winds hitting South America and the floods inundating Europe and Asia. Then it all changed and we got it as bad an anyplace in the world.

In the last two months, Pacific Northwest weather has been the worst in recoded history and totally unpredictable. Intense snowstorms are followed by record high temperatures that melt everything, causing landslides and floods. The forest is torn up out there, and now the snow is coming down again, driven sideways by 150 mph winds. Conditions can't get any worse, can they? It just has to get better. It just has to, with me being seven months pregnant. How could the climate change so fast, and what is going to happen next?

Oh God, please save my baby.

Chapter 5

Benitar Considers the Fates

Benitar Jackson hated to sleep.

Before the weather catastrophes that stormed through his every waking moment and thought, he used to be able to avoid bad dreams, by always awakening the moment one of his slumber stories went awry, as if an alarm had gone off in his head. Now each time he drifted off to sleep he went directly into a nightmare realm and could not escape from it, a plight that ran parallel to his conscious life.

"Get out of here!" he raged in a recurring dream, yelling at his entire seed-depository staff, and the intruder, Peggy Atkins. Holding a handgun inside the bunker, he heard the raging tempest outside, a war zone of ferocious winds, brilliant explosions of lightning and a cacophony of thunderous, shaking blasts, like bombs exploding.

Night after night, he had variations of this dream. In the most recent version he brandished the gun at them. "Get out or I'll shoot you! You don't appreciate what I'm doing here, what's at stake. You want to feed any animal that comes our way but I tell you over and over, we can't do that. Our lives only mean something if we save the seeds!"

In the dream, the faces of Abe, Peggy, and the others were frozen masks of fear. He opened the door and ordered everyone out, then slammed it shut and turned, thinking he was alone inside his precious seed bank. But a dozen children stood around him, all with the faces of the people he had just sent to their deaths. "Murderer," they whispered as they pointed at him. "Murderer!"

As if condemned to repeat the scene in various forms, Benitar Jackson backed against the door, and once more he seemed to feel the cold hardness against his backside. In the children, he saw hatred and loathing; their little faces were hard and purposeful, dancing toward him. "Call me what you want," he screamed, "but I can't feed all of you!"

"Murderer!"

Abruptly, Benitar awoke and sat straight up on his bed, rubbing his eyes in the darkness. "They don't understand," he moaned. "They'll never understand me."

Unable to return to sleep he remembered when he was a small boy, sitting with his father Avery Jackson on the bank of a river, watching the surface burn from a witch's brew that finally caught fire. His wealthy father had owned one of the many factories that lined the shores of an Ohio river, but one day he'd had enough of the hypocrisy, and began to wonder who was watching out for the quality of the environment around them. He became what the bosses called a turncoat, a whistle-blower to the media and the government, and it had cost him his job. Sadly, his warnings had come too late, and the fires had started anyway.

"Son," his father had said to him in the eerie glow from the surface of the river, "you can make a difference. This didn't have to happen. We live in a world where everyone thinks they can do as they please to the environment and it won't make any difference because it will never catch up with us. Each person is so small and insignificant, after all, and the world is so big. But what if that is multiplied by billions, and everyone behaves carelessly?"

Owing to his youth and inexperience, Benitar had not come up with an answer, and had just watched the river burn with its hypnotic glow.

"Promise me, my son, promise me that you'll make the world a better place than it was when you found it. Put yourself in a position to make a difference. The future will depend on you and people like you, to make up for the past." Despair had filled Avery Jackson's voice.

From that early age, as Benitar watched the oily red and yellow flames boil across the river, and saw the foul smoke smearing the evening sky, he had vowed not to let his father down. No matter what.

Now he found himself on a bed in the nightmarish, seemingly impossible future, a sweating and terrified man wondering how things had gotten so badly out of control, and if he could do anything at all to restore the balance. Sometime long ago, an American politician whose name he could not remember had said that extremism in the defense of liberty was no vice. The comment had made Benitar think, as he applied it to his own goals. Extremism in the defense of the seeds and the planet was no vice, either. He could, and should do anything to protect the seeds. Anything. He would kill every employee in the facility if they got in his way, and the desperate woman as well. His job would be a great deal harder if he had to go it alone, but he had the knowledge to perform every task they did, down to the last detail. He had made certain of that.

He had been hoping to keep this staff intact until the climate stabilized, but he didn't know when that would ever occur. If he died before they did, they might pervert his purpose, and he could not tolerate that. He couldn't fail his father.

In his ragged, fatigued mind, he was coming to the inescapable realization that one person had a better chance of saving the seeds than six. Thinking of Peggy Atkins, he felt a rush of rage. *Seven.* And if she gave birth: *Eight.* Benitar felt his jaw clamp and his body tense.

Why hadn't Abe allowed Peggy to die out there? The handgun sat on a table near the bed.

The seeds must survive at all costs, he though. *No matter what.*

And as he resolved to take the difficult next step, Benitar felt a distinct presence, as if his father was looking on and beaming approval on him, as if the son had finally pleased the elder, after all these years.

Benitar had to be exceedingly careful. While he had ordered executions, he had never killed anyone himself. Could he do it now, if it came to that? Yes, he thought he could, but wondered what it would be like to do that, to point the gun and—in the name of the future of life on the planet—shoot one person, and then another, and another. He couldn't leave them outside for animals to tear apart as he had done with others who stumbled into the area, couldn't risk having any of them get away.

Though filled with dread and guilt, Benitar felt absolute justification, that he would be remembered as the greatest hero in the history of Earth because he defended the last undamaged seed depository in the world—and the future it represented—against anyone who might threaten the heritage of millions of years of evolution. The future would honor him, if there was one, if the storms didn't destroy the facility, or if mobs didn't break in and take the precious seeds away … disasters that had befallen all of the other seed banks. He felt the tremendous weight of responsibility on his shoulders, and the skewering heat of his father's gaze on him.

The following morning, Benitar Jackson arose earlier than usual and went about his tasks at the Cascade Seed Repository, thinking of the gun in his lab coat, and of the extra clip of bullets he had brought with him this time. He had other firearms, too, hidden around the facility. Struggling internally, he delayed the inevitable and decided to await an excuse before "terminating" the staff, some incident to make the idea of killing more acceptable and sterile. Maybe it wouldn't have to be done. Maybe he could find another way.

But he couldn't think of anything, no matter how hard he struggled to come up with something—and time was running out.

Later that morning, at breakfast in the cafeteria, he saw Abe and Peggy gazing fondly at one another across a table in one corner.

"If necessary, I'll get them before they get me," Benitar Jackson said under his breath. He tightened his fingers around the gun in his pocket.

Chapter 6

Abe and Peggy Come to Know the Danger

Just before noon, Abe pushed open the door to Peggy's room, only opening it partway. He stuck his head through the opening and smiled. "How goes it?"

Peggy, moving her bed back into place against the wall, looked at him in surprise. "Oh—-"

"I'm sorry I startled you," said Abe. "If this isn't a good time ..."

She smiled. "It's OK. Come in."

Abe entered, and pushed the door closed behind him. She motioned toward a chair for him, and then sat lotus fashion on the bed. He turned the chair around and sat backwards on it, with his forearms resting on the top of the chair back. "Journal again?" he asked.

Peggy nodded, feeling the need to be honest with him, to trust him. "I don't think Benitar approves of our friendship," she said. "Did you see the way he was looking at us this morning?"

"I saw," Abe admitted.

"He's probably jealous, because no woman would have him. God, he gives me the creeps. I keep feeling like he'd like nothing more than to toss me out in the snow again."

"He wouldn't do that."

"Wouldn't he? You've really put yourself in a difficult position by helping me. I'm grateful but scared, and not only for myself and my baby."

The slender man scratched his chin thoughtfully. "He's just tired and stressed out, as all of us are. I really don't think …"

"Think again," Peggy said. Anyone who isn't one-hundred percent dedicated to saving the seeds is his enemy. I'm not contributing as a member of his staff, so in his eyes, I'm just in the way, taking food resources that he needs to complete his sacred task. I don't contribute around here, and when the baby is born it will be even more of a drain on resources, as he sees it."

Abe didn't say anything for awhile. Finally, he nodded his head slowly, and let out a long breath. "I don't want to think he would harm you or your baby."

"But he would, and you know it, don't you? Abe, you call him 'Top Seed,' but I think 'Bad Seed' might be more appropriate."

Abe rested his chin on his arms, which were still on top of the chair back. Presently he said, quietly, "I suppose I do sense something about him. I'm not sure. This seed repository has become his mission, his holy duty. You're very observant, picking up things about him quickly."

"I keep a journal, remember?"

He nodded.

"We've got to be discreet about whatever our friendship is," Peggy said.

"Or wherever it goes?" Abe asked, in a soft tone.

Peggy nodded. "Or wherever it goes." She smiled.

Carefully, quietly, he went over and sat on the bed next to her. "You going to be OK?" he asked.

She nodded, but she didn't feel OK.

"What did you write in your journal today?"

Pausing, Peggy smiled softly. "That you saved my life by rescuing me, even if it risked upsetting your boss. Without you, I'd have died out there alone in the cold, and my unborn child too, never even getting the chance to live. This morning I felt the baby move again, really kicking hard. Less than two months to go now, but born into what? Starvation? I feel so uneasy about bringing a child into this world. Earth is going to die soon, as we all are. My pregnancy is coming to term and I don't have a heck of a lot of choice here."

Her voice cracked with emotion, and trailed off. She cleared her throat, continued. "If I had only recently discovered the pregnancy, it might have been kindest to terminate. But that's not the way it is at this point; I can't do it now, not after getting to know my baby and her habits, even what she likes me to eat. I don't know why, but I think it's a girl."

"I wish I could say something to help you," he said.

She squeezed his hand. "You're helping me just being here."

"We live in a culture that makes women feel like monsters for wanting to abort a child," Abe said, "that killing a fetus is always wrong, even if the world into which the child is born is abusive and traumatizing, overwhelming her with so much fear that her brain can't develop properly."

"Here I am, bringing a child into a world that is dead," Peggy said. She stopped, her eyes welling with tears, then snuggled closer to him and rested her head against his shoulder, sobbing. "Oh God," she whispered, "what kind of world will my child be born into? Can it ever be like it was again? Will she have any sort of a chance?"

Abe put his arm around her shoulder and said, "I wish I knew, but I don't. Somehow, we need to have faith that what is happening, no matter how difficult, is meant to be. I know that sounds overly religious and all of that crud that lets people off the hook for being narrow-minded and cruel, but somehow we have to believe that it will all make sense in the end, that our lives have purpose."

Peggy took a long shuddering breath. She felt very vulnerable, and unable to protect her child. "Oh God, Abe, I wish I had your courage, your faith." She smiled. "You don't subscribe to any organized religion, but you're very spiritual."

Abe gave s short, nervous laugh. "You give me too much credit. I just try to be optimistic, to keep from going bug-bonging crazy."

In spite of her fear and grief, Peggy had to laugh with him.

Outside the door, Benitar Jackson heard their muffled conversation and laughter. He was not at all amused.

Chapter 7

Benitar Calls for Discipline

In his office afterward, Benitar Jackson wore a virtual-reality headset, which projected computer images in front of his eyes, e-mail messages from Conelrad and the news services to which he subscribed. For two days he had been operating in a news vacuum, since the messages weren't getting through. Finally, probably due to a break in the weather, the data was flowing again.

The news ranged from very bad to catastrophic, over much of the planet. A super typhoon with 310 mile per hour winds leveled half of the buildings in Hong Kong. A 90-foot tidal surge from a powerful storm wiped out Venice. Tornadoes had raged through New York, Washington D.C., and Philadelphia. Nearly a million additional people were dead or missing and presumed dead, in a matter of hours. An unconfirmed report was just coming in of a record-breaking hurricane hitting New Orleans, of dikes failing and half of the city underwater.

After absorbing the disturbing information, Benitar dictated a weekly staff bulletin summarizing the events, including his own updated orders. Then, sending a mental command through the VR headset, he transmitted the notice to four electronic bulletin boards around the seed repository.

Remaining in his office, he watched from a surveillance camera as four lunchtime diners in the cafeteria went over to the wall-mounted board and read it. Abe, Belinda, and Peggy were among them.

Suddenly, Peggy pointed at the screen and exclaimed, "Look! The words are changing!"

Using the camera, Director Jackson zoomed in on the screen, and to his horror he saw that a number of words were not what he had transmitted. Another electronic glitch, he thought at first. But he began to think otherwise, when Abe laughed, and said, "This is great. Can you believe what it says now?" The others laughed with him.

Then someone said, "Director Jackson doesn't have a sense of humor."

A murmur of concurrence went through the small group, and Belinda Amar glanced back at the surveillance camera, nervously.

In a mounting rage, Benitar focused on the perverted, blasphemous damage that a saboteur had done to the last three sentences of his message. In the original version, which he had on hard copy, it read:

We must all take the utmost care to safeguard the seeds, for they represent the future of humanity, the resurrection of the human species. I shall permit no dereliction of duty on my watch. If anyone violates my rules, there will be severe repercussions.

The perverted sentences were quite different, and he felt his blood pressure rise as he read them:

Don't bother to safeguard the seeds, for they represent nothing more than the demise of the human species. I shall permit no attention to duty on my watch. If anyone violates my rules, there will be no repercussions whatsoever, not even a spanking.

Even worse, the perpetrator had added a postscript:

Blow it out your alimentary canal, Director. And stop snooping on people.

Quickly, Benitar hit an override code, and darkened the bulletin boards entirely. Other than himself, there were five people in the facility, and three of them had been in the lunchroom at the time the changes appeared. He considered it unlikely, but not impossible, for any of them to have committed the atrocity. Of the two others who had not been in the lunchroom, he studied surveillance screens in his office to determine their whereabouts. Static filled one of the screens, providing no images, but the other screens showed the remaining employees at work.

All except Jimmy Hansik, whose record had been spotty at best. When he paid attention to his duties, he did passable, even good, work, but there had been noticeable lapses, and Jackson had come down hard on him. Could this be Hansik's way of getting even? He did have strong computer skills, but so did some of the other staffers. He wondered where Hansik was now, and why one surveillance screen had been filled with static. Had Hansik sabotaged that screen, as well as the bulletin?

For several moments, Director Jackson sat back in his chair and considered what to do next. He didn't feel especially close to any of his workers, and would just as soon wipe all of them out now. He had more than enough bullets to accomplish the task, and to his knowledge none of them had their own guns. But before doing that, he would like to know the identity of the traitor.

I must be discreet, he thought, *and not do the expected. I won't raise my voice to anyone about this, not at all. In fact, I'll act like it never happened. Maybe I'll even laugh about it. That will throw them off.*

Even so, I hate to do it. Maybe there's another way.

After calming himself with a sedative, Benitar checked the personal escape capsule that could only be accessed from his own room, via a private elevator. Sealed in a rooftop chamber over the bunker entrance, a chamber that he could enter by using keypad codes, the white, bullet-shaped capsule was just large enough for one person, and contained emergency food and water supplies, along with storage compartments holding a small quantity of the most important seeds in the world—enough to give plant life a new start somewhere.

It was his fallback plan, the one he didn't want to use, because it would mean abandoning the seed repository and giving up his life's work there, in favor of something smaller and more focused, of far less consequence. Of an ingenious design, the capsule would pierce the seemingly ever-present cloud cover and convert into a jet plane high in the air, an aircraft that anyone could operate, since it could be programmed to fly to any number of destinations and land safely. Once above the cloud cover, Benitar had the fuel range to reach the farthest points in the world, wherever he needed to go for the best chance of saving a sampling of the on-board seeds, and ultimately forming a new agricultural planting program.

After satisfying himself that the capsule was intact and in proper working order, he went down and made his normal rounds of the bunker, checking on the humidity, inspecting the seeds, tubers, roots, and bulbs, monitoring graphs and readouts … all the while feeling a sense of grim pride. He even smiled at two of the workers, and relished in the surprise that registered on their faces.

Yes, Benitar would save the precious stores, even if he had to deal with a slovenly crew of employees who didn't understand his methods. Entering Section D, he struggled to control his anger. His prime suspect, the bearded Jimmy Hansik was tending to the machines, intently making slight adjustments to the temperature and humidity settings. Five months ago, Hansik had been careless about this, causing some of the precious seeds to dry out. Now Benitar thought back and remembered the angry exchange between the two of them, with him yelling and Hansik standing there, looking defiant and defensive. At one point, the insolent employee had even said, "Benitar, don't blow a circuit over this. We have backup seeds for all of the ones we lost. It's not the end of the world."

Fuming and red faced, with his fists balled, Jackson had retorted: "It's exactly that if we don't protect the seeds, you fool, if you don't pay attention to our duties! Can't you comprehend what's happening to the weather, all the cities and towns that are being destroyed, the people that are being killed?"

To this, Hansik had just shrugged, asserting that the Director paid too much attention to the weather news. The employee's attitude had been so enraging that Jackson would have shot him on the spot, if he'd only had a gun with him at the time.

Now Benitar was ready for another confrontation with the man, more than ready for it, despite the sedative he had taken. "Did you hear about the tornado that destroyed Los Angeles?" he asked, and added, pointedly, "including your precious Hollywood? I guess you'll never get your big break in the movies now, so you won't get a chance to flex your overdeveloped muscles on the screen."

"I gave up on that long ago," Hansik said.

"Oh, really?"

"Yes, *really*." Hansik continued working as he spoke, went to his small desk and retrieved an electronic clipboard.

Smiling to himself, Jackson knew from eavesdropping with surveillance camera audios that this former body-builder had never given up the foolish hope that he would become an action hero one day. In one long, recorded conversation with Belinda, he had poured his heart out to her, over a bottle of wine.

"That's pretty funny what happened to my bulletin today," Jackson said.

"What's that?" Hansik looked up from the clipboard.

"Surely you heard. Someone changed my words around, making fun of me."

"A practical joke?"

"More like sabotage." Benitar studied Hansik's expression, didn't see anything there to assure him that this was the culprit. Whoever the fox was, Hansik or someone else, it would take some effort to bring it out of its hole.

Benitar touched the handgun hidden deep in his pocket, felt its cold, metallic smoothness, its potential for raw destruction. His forefinger caressed the trigger, and in his mind he saw himself opening fire on Hansik without warning, dropping him to the floor in a bloody heap. If he aimed carefully, Hansik wouldn't die right away, and he might be able to elicit a confession from him. But that was risky. Out of spite, the fool might not talk. Or he might be innocent.

Taking a deep breath, Jackson moved his finger away from the trigger, then whirled and stomped out into the corridor.

Chapter 8

Danger Lurks Out There

That evening, Belinda Amar and Jimmy Hansik lay close together after their lovemaking. She looked at him as he slept, the jet black hair, the Roman nose, the close-cropped dark brown beard. She'd seen pictures of him without the beard and he looked a lot better that way. Why did he have it now? She let her eyes admire his body, the tanned skin, the weight-lifter muscles. Belinda smiled to herself and wondered if he had also exercised the muscles involved with his sexual prowess.

She sniggered.

At the sound, Jimmy stirred. "Wha—huh—?"

Belinda shook her head. "Nothing." She still smiled.

Drowsily, Jimmy propped himself up on one arm and looked at her. "C'mon, wha's the joke?"

"Nothing." She blushed. "Just a girl thought."

Jimmy snorted, grinned. "About me?"

"Yes," she admitted.

"Well, I'm having boy thoughts about you. I wonder if they're similar."

"Could be, but I'm not talking."

"We didn't come here to talk anyway, did we?" He reached for her, but she pushed him away gently.

"It's not easy for me here," she said.

Jimmy's eyes narrowed. "Are you saying I'm not a good lover?"

"No, it's just that I miss my loft bed overlooking the blue waters of the Hood Canal and the snow-capped Olympic Mountains."

Jimmy flopped over on his back. "I know what you mean," he said, as if understanding suddenly. "It's difficult for me here, too. This isn't my bed with the surround-sound music system and a Jacuzzi in the other room." He closed his eyes, as if imagining.

Belinda stared glumly at the institutional beige walls of her tiny room, then up to the ceiling and the fluorescent lighting that had been dimmed by the removal of tubes to conserve electricity.

My God, she thought, *this sterile box has become my bedroom, my office, my world.*

She bit her lip, and memories flooded back of her life BTWB, her private code which stood for "Before Things Went Bad." She felt despair, grief, and anger, all rolled into one. She also knew why she and Jimmy were lovers now, when BTWB they acted as if neither of them really existed. It was all a matter of distraction, sensation, connection, and pleasure. Anything to deaden the pain, the loss of their former lives. Did her dream home even exist anymore or had it been smashed by a powerful tornado? Or buried in the huge blizzard that followed, crushed under the weight of snow?

If Belinda managed to get out of this, would there be anything for her to go back to? What about her Maine Coon cat Phylum, and her golden retriever Genus? A year ago, thinking she was going off to work on a typical day at the seed repository, she had left them at the house, and then had found herself trapped by the paranoia and unwavering commands of Benitar Jackson. Under an onslaught of weather, the Director, already precarious emotionally, had gone over the edge and taken the entire staff prisoner, threatening to shoot anyone who disobeyed him.

Like many forms of madness, Jackson's was rooted in reality. There really were catastrophes occurring out there, killing tens of millions of people all over the world, and maybe even more. But she resented the loss of her God-given right to free choice, and knew her co-workers felt the same way she did. She wasn't a religious fanatic like many survivors around the world, who had tilted like Jackson, sending them to the extreme end of ways they had already been leaning. She'd always had her own personal relationship with God, her own special prayers that had little to do with biblical texts or the sacred verses of any other organized religion.

She wondered if her beautiful little house on the canal was still standing, and if her beloved pets had long ago starved, or perhaps escaped … but to what? Maybe desperate, roving bands of people had shot Phylum and Genus for food. She felt a surge of nausea well up, and then slowly subside.

"What has happened?" she whispered to herself. "What has happened?"

For months now, she had studiously avoided looking into the mirror in her bathroom. She had even covered the glass with paper so that she wouldn't have to see herself with all her joy and purpose gone, the sallow skin, the lifeless blonde hair … as if even the color and sheen had been sucked away by the seed repository. It was as if the seeds themselves were using her energy as soil, taking away her life forces moment by moment, leaving her only a husk, a spent seed whose purpose was not to grow, but to give until there was nothing left to give.

"How did this happen?" she said louder than before, as if unaware of anyone else in the room.

"Pointless to ask that," Jimmy murmured, without opening his eyes. "We're here, and it's bad for now. Let's just be glad we have each other."

"But for how long?" she asked.

Jimmy sighed. He laid his right arm over his eyes, as if trying to block out the intruding light, and the awful reality it represented. "Try not to think about it," he said.

"I can't help wondering how much time we have left."

A long pause, then Jimmy said, "We're safe for awhile."

"I don't know," said Belinda.

"So the storms are worse than usual," he replied slowly, "but bad things have happened before, and the world always gets over it."

"Maybe not this time. One of these days we're going to run out of food," she said, "with no way of replacing it. We've all seen the expiration dates on the cans and other containers, and we keep eating the contents anyway because we're hungry. But we're risking illness—or worse."

"Finite resources, eh? You're starting to sound like our fearless leader."

"Don't mock me."

"It's bound to get better," Jimmy insisted. We're just having some weird and wacky weather, probably nowhere near as bad as the climate folks are saying. We're only hearing from the rabid environmentalists and obstructionists who can't make it on their own and expect government handouts. Well I say, if people can't take responsibility for themselves, they get what they deserve."

"You'd better have eyes in the back of your head," Belinda said.

"What do you mean?"

"You know how upset Benitar was over you not taking care of the seeds in section D. I don't think he ever got over it."

"That was months ago, so don't start. Just don't start. OK, I forgot to turn the humidity up but we had backup seeds to replace the ones that were lost."

Belinda looked at him coolly. "Just watch out for him, all right? He's more dangerous than ever."

Jimmy turned to look at her. "Don't go paranoid on me. We have a good time and you start going crazy with worry over me. I must be great in bed, eh?"

Belinda scooted up, pulling a blanket over her nakedness. "I'm not a nagging woman," she said, "just a friend, and I want you to listen. Benitar is on the prowl, and probably suspects you of sabotaging his bulletin. You're one of the three best computer operators we have, so you could have done it."

"I already told you, I didn't."

"And I don't know if I believe you." Touching his chin, she turned his face toward her, and he opened his eyes. "I know you're lying, Jimmy," she said. "Don't be surprised if Jackson has you on a hit list."

"Don't be so melodramatic. What's he going to do, kill me? He needs my skills and he knows it. Don't worry, Beautiful, this whole weather thing is cyclical and will blow over ..." He laughed at the unintentional pun, added. "Just look in the history books. We had a freaky weather thing happen, what, a century and a half ago when the volcanic island of Krakatoa blew itself to smithereens. They called it 'The Year Without A Summer,' and our Earth got over it. We're a resilient planet, and the same could be said of humans. That's why we've survived when other species have gone extinct."

"We made many of them go extinct, Jimmy. So it's only fitting that it might happen to us, too. The explosion of that volcano wasn't the same as the uncontrolled dumping of greenhouse gases into the atmosphere by industries and motor vehicles. Emissions have never been cut enough. Politicians with vested interests failed to act."

"So what do you want me to do about it? Take a huge shop vacuum and suck all the C02 and methane out of the atmosphere?"

"Don't be facetious," she said. "You need to take things much more seriously."

Jimmy turned on his side, away from her. "Yeah, yeah, Benitar's gonna shoot all of us. Sure, sure."

Belinda didn't say anything for a moment, as the very real possibility of that sank in. Then she said, "He didn't notice me today, when I saw him standing outside the door to Peggy's room, spying on her and Abe. He had his ear by the door, was listening to them."

For a moment, Belinda heard Jimmy's breath catch and she watched as he opened his eyes to look at the door.

"He could be out there right now," she said. A chill ran down her spine.

Chapter 9

Another Nightmare

Disbelieving, Benitar Jackson stared at the Conelrad report on the VR display that floated in front of his eyes. He sat in his windowless office, with its locked door visible to him beyond the projected images. It was late evening, and the fatigue of the day and all of his responsibilities weighed heavily on him.

So many problems, and none of them were small. Within the hour, he'd discovered that the exterior blast door was malfunctioning. He'd managed to close it with the manual override function, but it needed to be fixed. Another damned electrical problem that Jimmy Hansik hadn't dealt with.

To make matters worse, Conelrad's Environmental Crisis Department was reporting that weather conditions, as bad as they had been in recent months, were deteriorating even more, and precipitously. Major cities had either been isolated by the conditions or substantially destroyed. Forty-foot storm surges had taken out the remaining dikes in New Orleans, and the city was completely underwater. St. Louis had been devastated by a Category Five hurricane, with sustained winds of 230 miles per hour and gusts up to 280. Temperatures in Los Angeles and Phoenix were exceeding 125 degrees, and torrential rains had turned Death Valley into a lake.

Shaking with fear, Benitar felt lightheaded, as if from too much sugar or a spike of high blood pressure. He nearly passed out, saw the Conelrad report flicker in front of his eyes. Struggling to maintain consciousness, he closed his eyes for a moment and took a long, agitated breath.

When he looked again, he was able to read the VR words: "Impossible, given these conditions, to get any help to you. Could be worse where you are. At least you're not burning up like Australia with temperatures averaging 125 degrees or wiped out by rising seas like the Marianas Islands and other low coastal areas. It's difficult to tell how much worse it's going to get, but experts say we have a ways to go before any stabilization occurs. Wish we had some good news, but we don't. Protect the seed bank at all costs, and continue working on hybrids that will grow in extreme climatic conditions."

Benitar shuddered with fear, and asked himself, "What am I supposed to do?"

He switched off the virtual-reality screen and flipped the visor up, then rested his elbows on the desk and buried his face in his hands. Mentally, he did the math. Six people on the repository staff, not counting Peggy and her soon-to-be born child, could last maybe four and a half months. With two extra mouths to feed—if they cut back even more on rations—less than four months, considering that the baby would eat and drink less than an adult.

"Four months," Benitar whispered. "It's now October 31st, so the food will last until early March if we're lucky." He let his breath out slowly, and realized the irony.

Today was Halloween. Happy Halloween. Ghosts, Goblins, bats, werewolves, spiders, and the undead, all knocking on the door. He laughed weakly, bitterly, knowing he would trade the real versions of all of those monsters for the most frightening monster he had ever heard of, the weather.

A voice interrupted him, sounding as if it was coming from the VR headset he had switched off: "You have disappointed me."

Benitar opened his eyes and dropped his hands. As he did so, the virtual-reality visor flipped down over his face, and he saw the image of his father standing in front of him. The man was frowning. Feeling himself drawn into the field, Benitar Jackson no longer saw his office beyond it. He seemed to be inside the milieu, with nothing "virtual" about it. Seeing his father, he couldn't help believing it actually was him. Somehow he had returned from the dead, and not like one of the costumed trick-or-treaters of All Hallows Eve.

"I'm sorry …" he found himself looking beseechingly at his father. Though fifty-nine years of age, Benitar felt only eight in Avery Jackson's presence, never quite able to free himself of the parental anger and disapproval. "I'm s-s-sorry," Benitar said in a shaking, halting voice. "But I—I—did try to please you."

"Trying is not always enough." The dark eyes were piercing, unforgiving. "You could have made a fortune as I did and had the power to influence public policy."

"What could I have done differently? The world is in chaos, and I'm not to blame for that."

"The class you failed at Yale cost you the position I got for you in the Environmental Protection Agency, where you could have risen through the ranks and had the power to do something with your life. You could have made a real difference in the world, instead of the way you've ended up, with your back to the wall."

Benitar wilted under his father's disapproving stare. He hated that look. It made him feel so stupid, ashamed, and unworthy. "You weren't paying attention to my life. I was hired by the EPA, but they let me go because I was outspoken like you, criticizing the do-nothing administrators."

"You were fired for incompetence."

"Exactly the opposite. I was fired because I was *too* competent."

"Admit your own failures. Face them and take responsibility."

"Dad, you're not being fair to me."

Benitar watched his father turn and walk away, and in his path a burning river appeared, with flames flickering on the polluted water. Avery Jackson halted, oddly profiled against the orange glow of the fire. Putting his right hand up, he made a sweeping gesture across the scene, and the fire extinguished, leaving the waters of the river sparkling blue and clean and pure.

"Dad ..."

But Benitar's father walked out into the water, not once turning back to look, but continuing on until his head disappeared beneath the surface of the river.

Benitar cried out, a doleful wail for what he had lost, and what could never be again. He became aware of the virtual-reality headset, saw the visor fade from view. Reaching up, he felt it on top of his head, where he had earlier flipped it out of the way.

Did I only imagine it? he thought. *No, it had to be real. He came back to me, and he's watching me now.*

With fresh determination, Director Jackson pulled a gun out of his lab coat, and stared at the weapon.

"Dad," he whispered reverently, as if addressing a god, "you'll be proud of me yet."

With that, he took the gun and strode toward the door, knowing what he had to do next.

Chapter 10

An Accidental Meeting

"I've already named my child," Peggy said.

In Belinda's tiny room, she sat on the floor on a thick pillow, with her back supported by a wall. Belinda sat cross-legged in front of her, in the middle of the floor. A chess board was between them, with a game in progress, the third one they had played this evening, the tie-breaker.

"It's Rose," Peggy said. She smiled, and touched her stomach as it jumped. "Little Rosie is signaling that she's pleased to meet you."

"She has quite a kick. Look at that! How did you get a medical test to determine the sex?"

"Well, I just got back from the deep forest clinic, after waiting in line with the bears, the deer, and a couple of mama raccoons. No, silly. I just know it's a girl, that's all. And she's anxious to get out."

"We all are," Belinda said, in a dismal tone. "We're trapped in here because of people getting into power that had conflicts of interest—oil men for example, seeking to control oil-rich countries." She stared at the board, then moved a black pawn forward one square. The set had hand-carved wooden pieces and a board of inlaid fossil ivory.

Belinda was always railing against particular political leaders, but Peggy didn't completely agree with her point of view, which they had been debating during the game.

"It wasn't all the fault of our leaders," Peggy said now, responding to a diatribe by Belinda had just made against a series of U.S. presidents, who held power up to the time when the government collapsed and—pursued by angry mobs—went into hiding. "Global warming started long before they started passing the presidency around to each other," Peggy added. "The American public knew about it back in the 1970s, but we as a people have been in denial, continuing to drive big cars and consume as if there were no limit to the resources of this planet."

Shaking her head, Belinda said, "The politicians and their corporate cronies didn't do enough to stop global warming, and mounted disinformation campaigns that were designed to confuse the public. Citing potential damage to the U.S. economy, a succession of American governments refused to enter into agreements with other nations to reduce greenhouse gas emissions and take other environmental-protection actions. What a bunch of hooey. The politicians were using economic reasons as a smokescreen for what they wanted to do, what would line their pockets with greenbacks."

"You seem to overlook facts that don't support what you want to believe."

"Such as?"

"Such as the fact that China, India, and other countries were exempted from any potential agreements. That isn't right. Why should America join if China—with its huge rate of industrial growth—wasn't participating?"

"The U.S. should have made itself an example for the world," Belinda insisted. "A good one, instead of a bad one. I trace all of our problems back to our self-aggrandizing presidents and their cronies. Remember the two Iraq wars, fought for oil interests? And the trillion-dollar mineral deposits in Afghanistan—do you really think that had nothing to do with us sending our forces in there, and keeping them there?"

"I came here to play chess, not to solve all the problems of the world," Peggy said, feeling increasingly irritated. Peggy's own father and mother had been lifelong Republicans, working for state and national congressional candidates, so she had heard all the arguments at the dinner table.

"Have it your way," Belinda said, with a tight smile. "But while you're thinking of your next move, I'll just say one more thing. The real war our country should have fought was against industrial and auto emissions. Now we're fighting a different kind of a war, against Mother Nature … and we can't defend ourselves against her power."

Peggy castled her king, a defensive move. "I feel guilty for bringing Rosie into such a bleak world, but I can't abort her."

"You Republicans are all alike," Belinda said. Quickly, she moved her queen across the board diagonally, an attack that paralleled the aggressiveness of her political arguments.

"I remember when snow was a beautiful thing," Peggy said, ignoring the attempt to draw her into more debate. "I would have liked to have taken Rosie out to build a snowman, like in the old days … seeing her laugh at falling snowflakes and sled down a hill. Then in the spring, with the thawing of ice and snow, I would have shown her how to put seeds into the earth, all the wonder and magic of making young flower shoots come up from the ground."

"The old days are gone forever."

"At least we agree on that."

"I can't remember the last time I saw the sun," Belinda said.

Peggy heard two raps at the door, and it swung open. Jimmy Hansik stood there holding two large bottles of wine, one in each hand. Abe Tojiko was right behind him.

"We were rifling through some lockers and there was this dirty lab coat on the bottom of one and it looked bulkier than it should have been and lifting it up, we found these bottles of champagne."

Belinda took one of them from him, and studied the label. "A reserve Piper Heidsieck," she said. "Expensive stuff, imported from France. Which locker?" She frowned, looking suddenly suspicious.

"One of them by the front stairway."

"No name on the locker?" Belinda asked.

"Nope."

"Hey, Peggy," Abe said. He kneeled by her, examining the chess board. "Who's winning?"

"Don't ask."

"No name on the lab coat?" Belinda asked.

Jimmy shrugged. "If there was, I sure didn't see it. Besides, the locker was unlocked."

Belinda frowned again. "Well, a lot of us never lock our lockers, and no one takes anything."

"Until now," Jimmy said. "Think of it this way. Whoever hid this stuff has been holding out on us."

"He has a point," Abe said. "The way this world is, who knows how long we have left, and we don't want good champagne going to waste. Pop one open, Jimmy."

Jimmy looked with utter glee at the bottle he still held, as if it was a big game trophy. He checked the door of the room, made sure it was closed. Putting the bottle between his knees, he removed the stopper with a loud "pop!" that startled Peggy, a noise that caused her baby to kick.

Foam gushed out of the bottle. "Whoa!" Jimmy said, putting his mouth around the opening. Then, lowering the bottle after the foam subsided, "Good stuff. Maybe I'll keep this one for myself."

"Hand it over," Abe said. He glanced around. "Any glasses or cups in here?"

"No," Belinda said. "Let's just pass it around." She set the unopened bottle on a table. "I suspect we're going to get into this one, too."

Abe took a long sip. "Mmmm." He extended it toward Peggy.

"No thanks," she said. "I have the baby to think about."

"Oh, right. Probably not a good idea, because your nutritional status is already compromised."

Abe handed the bottle over to Belinda, who swigged it like a wino on a park bench.

"You're all drinking too fast," Peggy said. "Slow down, or you'll make yourselves sick."

"She's right," Belinda said. She took a small sip and appeared to savor it, holding it in her mouth for a long time.

As Peggy watched her three friends share the first bottle and open the second, the drinkers began to relax and chat as if they had no troubles in the world. She felt good for them; this was an unexpected luxury, a chance for them to escape from all of the pressures. She began to take part in the banter, laughing with them and beginning to calm down herself, just a little.

"*In vino veritas*," Peggy said, as she watched them share the second bottle. "In wine there is truth."

"Don't get serious on us," Abe said. He was holding his wine pretty well, but Belinda was becoming quite giddy, and giggling more than talking.

After awhile, Abe said, looking wistfully at one of the wine bottles as he passed it to Belinda. "Maybe we should have shared this with the rest of the staff."

"A little late for that," Jimmy said. "Besides, how do we know who owns the stuff? If we'd gone public with it, who knows who would have said what?"

As Belinda drank more, her cheerful mood didn't hold. She started to express anger toward Jimmy for his behavior, what she called his "attitude of entitlement," in which he claimed to deserve the breaks, while no one else did. Peggy wasn't sure what she meant by that or what had set her off. Jimmy continued to drink and ignored her.

"I can't believe I slept with you," Belinda finally said. "You self-centered maggot."

That got his attention, and he hurled the nearly empty first bottle of champagne against a concrete wall, smashing the glass.

"I'm not used to this much alcohol," Belinda said. She pushed the remaining champagne bottle away when Abe tried to hand it to her. "It's been so long since I drank like this. I think I just need to be by myself for the rest of the evening."

"Izzat an apology?" Jimmy asked, slurring his words.

"Not quite, maggot," she said.

"Well, I don' wanna be by myself," Jimmy said. "As a matter of fact …" He reached around and tried to grope her chest, but she gave him a hard cuff on the cheek.

Undaunted, he leaned over and pressed his mouth against her neck in a sloppy kiss.

Again, she pushed him away, "No—" She got up and opened the door, unconsciously brushing her hair back.

Rising to her feet, Peggy said, "This party's over." She met Abe's inquisitive gaze, saw the desire in his eyes. Seeing her look of disapproval, Abe broke his gaze with her.

In apparent disbelief, Jimmy looked at Belinda for a long minute, his eyes trying to focus on her, seemingly unaware of just how much the champagne was affecting him, too. At length, he got up, grabbed the unfinished bottle, and walked to the door, with Peggy and Abe following him into the corridor.

Jimmy tried to take a swig while he was walking, but stumbled and fell against a rack of laboratory glass that had not yet been put away. Flasks, beakers, and Petri dishes cascaded, breaking on the floor.

The champagne bottle went flying out of his hands and smashed into pieces—at Benitar Jackson's feet.

Chapter 11

Showdown

Benitar Jackson stared in disbelief at the scene before him: at Jimmy, sprawled in the middle of broken glassware, at Belinda, clutching the door frame of the room … and at Abe and Peggy behind her. After hesitating for a long moment, the Director reached into his coat pocket and pulled out the handgun.

"Oh, my God," whispered Belinda, "Benitar, don't!"

"Damn you to hell, Hansik," Jackson said, waving the gun at him. "You kill the seeds, you stomp around here like a god damned entitled know it all, you steal my champagne and you probably don't even know that the blast door is malfunctioning. Did you know I had to shut it with manual override? Where in the hell are your priorities?"

Stupidly, Hansik looked up Benitar. His mouth worked, and after a struggle the slurred words came, "An assi-den' Benitar, we g-got to t-toastin' the-the seeds and you, and …" Finally, the obvious lies failed and his mouth worked soundlessly, as if a puppet master was pulling the string.

"What's wrong with the blast door, you idiot? Is it another electrical problem that you can't figure out?" In Benitar's own ears, his voice sounded low and mean, and for a moment he was struck by the irony of it, since that was how his father used to sound whenever he drank too much and got nasty. But the awareness did not diminish his rage. "You've been the bane of my life since I was foolish enough to hire you. You never gave a damn about the seeds. This has never been more than a job to you, has it?"

"Ish losh more ta me. Your sheeds are criddigal ta me."

"They are not *my* seeds, you fool! They belong to the people of the United States, and to the world. I am merely the custodian."

"I'm sh-shorry. Of c-course, I meant that."

Tilting his head in disdain and staring down the bridge of his nose, Benitar said, "You are totally without honor."

"I'll clean this mesh up," Hansik said, rising to his feet.

"I'll make my father proud of me yet," Benitar vowed, "and you won't get in my way." He pointed the gun at Hansik, then looked around, at the others.

"Le' me make it up," Hansik said, picking up some of the larger pieces of broken glass and forming a pile on one side.

"I've had it with all of you," Benitar said, "and I'm starting with you first, Jimmy, you little weasel. The more of you I kill, the more food there will be for me, so I can make sure the seeds are saved."

Bravely, Belinda inched out into the hallway, closer to the Director. "I know you're upset sir, and rightfully so, but please don't hurt anybody. It's not worth it, solves nothing ..."

As if in a dream, Benitar heard the delicate clinking of the glass shards as Jimmy moved on the floor and noticed the cuts on his hands, now oozing with blood. It was an odd sensation, making Benitar feel he was somehow apart from the scene, watching it all, seeing the gun in his own hand and all he had to do was pull the trigger, getting rid of a mouth to feed that belonged to this worthless Jimmy Hansik.

And slowly, he became aware of someone else.

"No, Director Jackson," Belinda said. "Please put the gun down. It was just an accident. Jimmy and Abe had no way of knowing the champagne was yours. The locker was open, with no name on it. They didn't know it belonged to you."

"It belonged to somebody, didn't it?" His gazed flickered over to Abe Tojiko, a hard glare that reflected the portion of the blame he was assigning to each of them.

"They didn't know that," Belinda said. "They must have thought it was abandoned by some former employee."

With an abrupt jerking movement, Benitar pointed the weapon at her, and now he cocked it. "You're in on this too, and the champagne was mine, saved for a special occasion. The bottles were wrapped in a lab coat, with my name on the lapel."

"Didn' shee that," said Jimmy, still making clinking noises with the glass. "Didn' know it was yours an' we're sh-shorry Benitar, didn' see your name onna lab coat. Abe and I'll go out and buy you shum more as shoon azza weather clears."

Benitar watched Jimmy as he tried to keep from falling down again. His balance was precarious, and he had to hold onto the wall. The cuts were deep on his forearms, and blood dripped on the floor, a further violation. Benitar always insisted on clean floors in the Cascade Seed Repository.

The barrel of the gun moved again, and this time it pointed directly at Hansik's heart, as if the weapon had a brain of its own and would decide whom to kill, and when.

"P-please," Hansik said. His skin had gone pale, and his eyes were open wide, causing Benitar to smile. He could stand there forever and enjoy this incompetent employee's fear, such a minuscule payment for all the grief he had caused.

Slowly, he became aware of Belinda again, as she said, "It's OK, Director. When we're out of this we'll buy you a whole case of French champagne, but you have to put the gun down ..."

"I'm so glad you're going to replace the champagne," Benitar said. "As soon as the weather gets nice and warm and everything is the way it used to be, everyone in the world can have French champagne again.

Will this weather ever get any better?" he asked, plaintively. "Will it ever get any better?"

"Of course it will," a woman said. He saw her through glazed eyes. Strangely, it looked like Peggy Atkins. How did she dare talk to him? The gun barrel found her, emerging into the corridor from the room, with her oversized harlot-belly. Abe was with her, getting in front of her, as if he could stop a bullet intended for her. But Benitar could shoot both of them, maybe even with one shot that went through both of them. Three of them at once, actually, including the bastard child.

Peggy had been watching the scene in horror, afraid for herself and for her child, afraid this madman would cut loose and kill all of them. Finally, she could bear it no more. She had to make her own attempt to get through to him, because Belinda wasn't getting anywhere, and their boyfriends were paralyzed, impotent with their own fear. Now Abe, impressing her, was moving to intervene. It all seemed like a dream to her, a horrible nightmare.

Moving closer, after pushing Abe aside insistently, Peggy extended a hand to the distraught Director, and said, "We all admire your dedication to duty, but you're tired, and you need our help, if you'll let us. Let *me* help you." She stood right next to him now, and looking up, Peggy saw the glazed, confused look on his face. "Give me the gun, sir."

"I never realized how pretty your hair is," Benitar said with a soft smile, "and how deep blue your eyes are. Funny how you can see someone day after day but not really see them." His gun wavered.

Then he lurched, and jammed the gun barrel against Jimmy Hansik's head, right between the eyes. "Thought I forgot about you, didn't you?"

"No, Benitar," Hansik pleaded, sounding suddenly sober, "No, please no! I'll do whatever you say. Just give me a chance."

"Oh, I so love it when you plead, little Jimmy scum." His finger tightened on the trigger....

56

Chapter 12

The Beginning of the End

Blam! Blam! Blam! Blam! Blam!

Silence. Followed by a loud *crash*.

Anxiously, Benitar looked up a stairway toward the blast door that led outside. Incomprehensibly, the huge door shook.

Peggy grabbed Benitar's gun hand.

He cursed at her and pulled away.

Crash! Crash!

The door to the repository slammed open. A haggard figure appeared in the doorway, with shadowy shapes beyond, on the moonlit snow. Someone yelled, "Food! Get the food inside!"

Benitar aimed and fired three times.

Two of the intruders fell, and tumbled partway down the stairs. A panicky voice yelled from outside, "Run, they've got guns!"

Benitar, Belinda, and Jimmy ran up to the heavy door, stepping over and around the bodies that bled in the snow drift, amidst freezing sleet on a night wind. Shivering, the Director saw a dozen people outside, slogging through the snow in the moonlight, trying desperately to get away.

He fired until his clip was empty, and dropped four more of them on the snow, not paying any attention to Belinda or Peggy behind him, who tried to get him to stop. The other figures disappeared into the shadowy woods before he could snap in the second clip. The moon, seen as rarely at night as the sun was in the daytime, shone through a thinning cloud cover.

Abe and Jimmy secured the door, reinforcing it from the inside with planks and nails that Benitar brought out.

Peggy Atkins shook her head as she crouched by the bodies, examining them. "Boys," she said bitterly, "—just boys."

Belinda, Jimmy, and Abe stared, while Peggy wept softly.

Benitar Jackson sighed. "The ones that got away will be back, with more. They'll keep battering us, but they have to get through that narrow entrance, and I'll fight them with everything I've got." He paused. "I have more guns, you know."

Abe nodded slowly. Then he gave the Director a long, beseeching stare. "What if they bring their own guns next time, Benitar? What if men come, not just boys? Some of them may be seeking revenge."

To Benitar, the tone had a dull, leaden chill to it. The questions made the situation bluntly clear to him, and crystallized the challenge he faced here, and the enemies he had to overcome.

Benitar looked at the bodies on the stairs, then at Abe, Belinda, and Peggy. Finally, he glared at Jimmy Hansik, who had bloodied hands and glass shards on his clothing.

Abe said again, slowly, deliberately, "Well what about it, Benitar? What happens next?" Now he spoke in a condescending, scolding tone, as if addressing a child who had misbehaved.

Feeling oddly detached, Benitar snapped a new clip full of bullets into his gun. The hand that held the weapon seemed to take on a life of its own, and he realized that he could only follow it, doing its sacred bidding. For several moments the hand pointed the barrel randomly — up, down, back, forth, and to the side as if the hand was acting independent of Benitar's consciousness and whatever it did was not the Director's fault.

To him, it seemed that one direction was as good as another, and one was as useless as another. He walked down the stairs to the main floor of the seed repository, stepping past the bodies, then continued down the hallway and into his own room, where he quietly closed the door behind him.

In shock and dismay, Peggy and her companions stared after him. Finally Peggy, with a hand on her pregnant belly, said in a soft, plaintive tone, "Boys. They were just boys—."

Chapter 13

Dreams and Responsibilities

It was the far side of midnight when Abe, Jimmy, Peggy, and Belinda wrapped up the bodies in orange plastic bags and put them in the freezer section of a cavernous cooling chamber that was used for food storage and the preservation of certain seeds, as well as tubers, roots, and bulbs. As they completed the grim task, no one spoke, but Peggy thought of the others who had fallen outside, and wished she could go out and check on them. But she was pregnant and couldn't take such a risk. Besides, it would endanger the seed bank, making it even more vulnerable to attack. She hated thinking like Benitar Jackson, a man who would do anything to advance his cause, a man whose ethics were laced with violence.

After closing the door to the cooler, Peggy and Abe parted company, each going to their own small sleeping quarters. Belinda and Jimmy went into the room where they had been co-habiting.

As Belinda Amar drifted off to sleep, she dreamed that she was back in her house again, overlooking Hood Canal. It was a cool, cloudy day like so many others, and she had a good fire going in the green, ceramic-framed fireplace. Her cat Phylum purred beside her on the couch, while her golden retriever Genus snoozed on the floor.

Looking up from a book on her lap, Belinda gazed around her wonderful little Victorian home, at the expensive art on the walls, and then looked out the window at her classic old Mercedes coupe, parked at the curb in front. She felt fortunate to have so much, and was proud of herself for having earned it all. Her life was perfect, almost untarnished. Focusing back on the book, however, the words began to vanish, sentence by sentence. Anxiously, she turned the pages, one after the other, but all of them were the same, with vanishing words.

The book slipped from her grasp, thudded onto the floor. Beside her, Phylum had died, and was rotting before her eyes, a horrendous death in fast forward. Belinda shrieked, jumped up, and felt her heart beating wildly. She wanted to run, but through the window she saw something dark and foreboding approaching from a distance. A storm? She also realized that the waters of Hood Canal had turned to ice, and suddenly she understood.

Stepping back from the window, she saw a massive glacier, like a high, flat, white beast rushing toward her, slabs of ice breaking off the front as it moved. Dazed and helpless to move out of the way, she watched it come toward her, and heard a rumbling, thunderous noise. In a matter of seconds the glacier towered over the small community, crushing everything in its path....

Beside her, Jimmy Hansik was caught in his own nightmare. He found himself on a tarmac, hurrying toward a large passenger plane that awaited him, with its engines running, Abruptly, Jimmy paused in his headlong rush, as the plane became like a mirror, and on the hull he saw a vision of blue sky and lazy, drifting clouds. Over the whine of the engines, he heard women laughing and an eerie roar of surf, and he saw an oversized reflection of himself in the glassy surface, waving and yelling, "C'mon, c'mon, climb aboard before it's too late!"

"I'm coming," Jimmy yelled. But as he ran, he noticed a curious gray cloud forming before him, a cloud that suddenly mushroomed in height and width, and enveloped him. Instantly, he felt the blinding, freezing sting of a blizzard, and he thought, *This can't be happening to me! It can't possibly be.*

An indeterminate time passed, with no sensations whatsoever. The next thing he realized the storm had abated and he was buried up to his neck in snow. Struggling to break free, he realized to his dismay that he was frozen in place, and only his eyes could move. Suddenly the whine of the jet became a deafening roar and again he saw his previous reflection in the glassy surface of the jet, looking stricken and yelling at him. "What are you waiting for? You're going to miss your plane! It's all you've ever wanted."

Jimmy tried to yell that he was coming, but the words iced up in his brain and his mouth was frozen solid, open and filled with snow. In helpless horror, he watched the plane taxi away from him slowly. "Wait!" he wanted to yell, but he could make no sound. Tears came and solidified instantly, and the last thing he saw before his eyes froze shut was that magnificent aircraft picking up speed, lifting off, and vanishing into the serene and clear blue sky....

Abe, in his private room, sat at a table, resting his arms on the surface. Feeling despondent, he put his head down on the folded arms and ceased trying to think. Instead, he just let his thoughts drift, wherever they wanted to go....

His long-dead grandmother, Sophie, came back to him in a vision, her dress and hair blue flames, her eyes yellow. She hovered large before him, as she had in his younger life. "You're way too soft-hearted," she said, "shouldn't have brought Peggy Atkins in from the snow. It only aggravated Director Jackson, tipped the poor man over the edge."

Abe saw himself as a child again, afraid to speak to this immense and imposing woman, cringing in her presence and staring at her beefy hand, the one she always used to strike him. Somehow, the words came to him now, for the first time in his life. "I'm not frightened of you anymore, you domineering old hag, and I saved Peggy because it was the right thing to do."

"You think you're in love with her. Is that it?"

"What business is it of yours?"

"Abe, foolish boy, when will you ever listen?" Grandmother Sophie's eyes blazed hatred and utter contempt. Her mouth, when she opened it to scold him, was like looking into a glowing, volcanic vent. He couldn't remember her ever saying anything nice to him, not a single time in all the years he knew her, before she died of a well-earned heart attack. She always made him feel bad about himself, and he realized now that she did that to justify her own miserable existence, so that he would need to depend on her.

At long last, Abe saw himself standing firm against his bête noire, finding the strength he never had before, and he said, "I have no time for you, Grandmother. The world is dying and I refuse to die a coward, or without ever knowing love. Fly away on your broomstick, witch, and never come back!"

Grandmother Sophie hissed, and yellow flames shot from her mouth, but Abe did not move. In spite of his fear, he did not flinch. And before his eyes, Sophie burned like an incandescent candle— bright blue, yellow and orange—and incinerated herself, since Abe's fear no longer provided fuel for her evil spirit.

Relieved, Abe lifted his head from the table and thought, *Even now, at the end of the world, it's not too late to find courage and love.*

Closing his eyes again, he felt the tears for all that might have been. Finally, he got up, went to the bed, and drifted into a dreamless, yet profoundly calm, slumber....

In the pitch darkness of her room, Peggy felt overwhelming exhaustion. On her bed, she leaned back against pillows, and studied the color behind her closed eyes. Pitch black. She tried to visualize something about the future, tried to imagine what it might be like … if any human being had a future. But her mind wanted to go in another direction.

She recalled being in California, standing on a rocky promontory by the coastal highway, gazing out at the endless sea. But as she tried to bring back details of the scene, the familiar blue of the ocean became black, as did the flowers on the hillside around her and the green grasses. Looking up to the sky, she beheld a baroque sun, with stylized yellow and orange flames slowly curling up and out from the disk, burning in a black sky. As she watched, the moon eclipsed the sun, forming a brilliant corona, but when the eclipse ended she saw to her horror that the sun was dying.

Peggy wept softly, then drifted into a troubled sleep.

Chapter 14

She's So Small and Thin

Children are not always born at the most opportune of times, nor in the best of circumstances. So it was for the young mother Peggy Atkins, when her baby decided to make its big push for life in the middle of the night. The first thing Peggy realized as she slept was that she felt wet, and she dreamed she was being drenched under a cloudburst, in one of the warm summertime storms that used to occur in the Pacific Northwest, before the eternal snows came.

But as she lay in bed, layers of consciousness began to unfold in her mind, and she became aware of something confusingly wrong. Rain? Was the weather making a turn for the better? But she wasn't outside. Abe Tojiko had taken her into the seed bank.

As her awareness increased, Peggy worried about her baby, and she realized she was lying in a wet bed, with her nightclothes saturated. Startled, she tried to sit up, but stopped when she felt a lance of pain in her abdomen.

My baby!

She cried out, and screamed for help. Excruciating pain. She couldn't stop it, couldn't slow the baby down....

Not long afterward, Peggy held little Rosie in her arms, snuggling the child close in its improvised swaddling blanket, a thick white towel. Belinda Amar stood by her, having helped with the birth. Belinda, whose mother had been a registered nurse, had the most medical knowledge in the facility, but said now how grateful she was that there had not been problems, or she might not have been able to handle them. Little Rosie, as if unafraid of the world that lay outside the comfort and protection of her mother's womb, had surged forward efficiently, making her head-first plunge into the unknown. It had been left to the women to just cut the umbilical cord and tie it.

But Peggy's elation was short-lived, as she looked at her child with the new scrutiny of a concerned mother.

"She's so small and thin," Peggy said.

"Yes," Belinda said, "you'll need to give her as much natural milk as you can."

On the morning of the fourth day after her birth, little Rosie slept fitfully beneath a towel, inside a wooden box that Abe had painted white. She was not doing well, and Peggy felt increasing agitation and frustration at her inability to do much for her.

The young mother's breasts were still sore from a feeding an hour before, and she hadn't gotten used to having to wake up constantly in the middle of the night to keep the sick, irritable baby from crying. Now, despite her fatigue, Peggy couldn't sleep because of worry. She had produced milk from her own body, but wondered if it was enough, and if it had all the nutrients her helpless child needed.

Peggy didn't know how she found the energy to continue, since it was all so exhausting, but she knew she had to, for the sake of her beautiful, innocent daughter. So sweet and frail she was, and Peggy loved her dearly, though she hated the world into which Rosie had been born. So many times in the few hours of Rosie's life, Peggy had held her close and cried. Now, she felt an overwhelming wave of sadness come over her.

Wiping tears from her eyes, Peggy reached behind the bed and brought out her journal, then sat cross-legged on the blankets to write in it. She wanted to get down her feelings for Abe, and especially for the baby. What a miracle the little person was, clinging to life each day, showing her grit and determination.

Moments after the delivery, Belinda had said Rosie looked premature, and Peggy had done the math herself. Never having seen a doctor during the pregnancy, she couldn't be certain, but Rosie might have been two or three weeks premature. Now, she might be a few ounces heavier than her birth weight; Peggy hoped so, and prayed it was not just her imagination.

Following a moment's hesitation, she began to write in red ink, but opened with another subject, before getting to Abe and Rosie: *November 28th. This may be the last Thanksgiving any of us celebrate, without any turkey, cranberry sauce, or pumpkin pie. The ones who want to break in have been back every day, pounding on the bunker and testing the perimeter, looking for weak spots and dodging bullets fired at them by Director Jackson and other men he's allowed to have guns. After the first bloody event, our defenders haven't hit any of them, as the outsiders are being more careful.*

They have been taunting Jackson by name, making him even more of a madman than he already was, even more paranoid. The Director stays in his room with his guns all day, brooding, and emerging whenever the bunker is under attack, as he storms out and opens fire. It's become predictable, and I'm afraid I'm not the only one who's noticed. The outsiders must be charting him, working up a new plan to penetrate the minimal security we have. So far, they haven't shown any weapons, but that doesn't mean they can't get them.

Looking over at her sleeping baby, Peggy worried more than ever that her precious child was not safe in the seed depository. Sooner or later ... She tried not to imagine the horrible possibilities, didn't want to commit the worst of them to the pages of her journal.

While Peggy was giving birth to Rosie, the outsiders had made one of their attempts to break in, creating a lot of noise, but not getting through.

She knew that Benitar was beside himself trying to imagine the ways his enemies might get in, and he was increasingly desperate in his attempt to accomplish what he thought was his holy mission in life, protecting the seeds at all costs. The upper chamber where he kept what he called the "emergency seed evacuation capsule" was yet another weak point against intrusion, because the chamber had an escape hatch in the thick concrete roof—so he must be checking on it constantly.

But the existence of such a capsule—which the Director supposedly paid for himself—made no sense to the rest of the staff in the repository, because the whole facility was in a bunker, supposedly impregnable against atomic attacks. In reality, the aircraft had to be a personal escape capsule for Jackson, capable of transporting him (and perhaps a sampling of seeds) away for whatever reason he deemed necessary.

Despite all of the efforts and concerns by Benitar and his crew, Peggy didn't sense anything holy or sacred about this bunker. Rather, she felt the stench of evil all around, a dark and foreboding presence trying to sneak and batter its way in, intending to kill and destroy everything. She and Rosie were in the worst possible place, facing tremendous danger.

That morning, Benitar had distributed handguns to Abe and Jimmy. At least that was a small step in the right direction, Peggy thought. But a few guns and limited ammunition against a mob intent on breaking in? It was only a matter of time before they broke through that defective blast door again. The beleaguered defenders didn't have enough firepower to keep them out forever.

As the young mother paused over her journal, she became aware of tears falling on the open page, smearing the red ink. The image of Abe came to her, and she thanked God for him. She knew he loved her, not out of desperation, but because he really felt that way, even though he had not put it into words yet, undoubtedly because the continuing crisis prevented clear thinking processes and commitments. She wondered if she loved him herself, but likewise she had not uttered the words, had not dared to do so under the circumstances. It was like a war zone around here, forcing personal relationships to the wayside.

Finally she put some of her feelings for Abe on the page, then set the pen down and pushed her notebook aside. What a dismal, dead-end place this was to finally discover love, when it was so ephemeral and she couldn't enjoy it fully. And how unfair it was to her baby.

She whispered to her sleeping child, "I wish I could promise you a long life, but I cannot. I can only assure you that you have been born into love, and I will protect you for as long as I can. That is all a mother can offer you, and hopefully in the end it will be enough. Oh, Rosie how I wish I could promise more."

Sapped of energy, she lay back on the bed and closed her eyes. Presently, the baroque vision of the stylized sun came over her again, followed by the moon eclipsing it. But this time the corona burned and flared suddenly with ferocious brilliance, like a final burst of energy from a dying sun.

Chapter 15

The Escape Capsule

Hearing a tremendous commotion outside his room, Abe yanked open the door and hurried into the corridor, carrying the silver-and-black .38 pistol that the crazed Director had given to him. He had heard these sounds before, and knew it was another attempt to get in.

Abe raced to the bottom of the staircase and looked up at the door, reinforced with heavy planking nailed from the inside. Would it hold this time? To his horror, he saw the thick barricade shake more than ever before, from repeated blows on the other side.

He became aware of people around him, including Benitar Jackson, who put a foot on the bottom stair and pointed another handgun up at the door. "They can't get in!" he shouted, but he didn't sound confident. His dark gaze darted around wildly. The man had the look of madness about him.

Abe scratched an itch on the back of his neck, felt a raw spot from a nervous habit he had developed in recent days. "I pray that you're right, but prayers don't seem to offer much protection anymore."

Belinda joined the others, and down the corridor Abe saw Peggy standing in her own doorway, a rare moment when the doting mother wasn't holding her baby or otherwise tending to it. "There must be something else we can do," Belinda said. She looked distraught, and Abe knew why. Only an hour ago, Jimmy Hansik had been found dead in one of the storerooms, apparently poisoned by botulism in a can of salmon. Under the circumstances, with no real doctor in the seed repository, the answer might never be known. Rumors were swirling that Director Jackson had murdered him, and made it look like an accident.

Abe thought the truth was that some of the cans were outdated, and Jimmy took a chance and lost. Everyone had seen the cans and the expiration dates on them, even slight bulges in some cans that didn't seem to harm anyone when they ate the contents. It had been going on for months, and Jimmy just got unlucky.

At Abe's side, Benitar continued to stare up at the door as it shook, but continued to hold. Gradually the commotion outside died down, and the repository staff dispersed, murmuring uneasily among themselves.

Abe stood in the corridor with Peggy. "Are you getting any sleep?" he asked. Looking up at him, she saw that his face was a strange, anguished mask.

Shaking her head, she confessed, "Not much. I was just dozing off, trying to take a nap when I heard all the racket." Behind her, she saw that Rosie had fallen into a more peaceful sleep, despite the nearby noise.

Peggy noticed Abe's deep concern that showed in his voice and his unconscious mannerisms, especially in the nervous twitching around his jaw. He still held the .38 pistol, had it pointed at the floor.

"This is awkward for me to say," Peggy began, "but I'm afraid I'm not producing enough milk for Rosie. Can you bring me some powdered milk?" She felt a deep, rising panic.

Grimly, Abe nodded.

Hearing Rosie stir, Peggy hurried to her and lifted her out of the makeshift crib. So light in her arms. She tucked the towel around Rosie's tiny form, and saw the sickness from malnutrition in her blue eyes, a malady that seemed to be getting worse.

"Something else you should know, I guess ..." Abe followed her into the room and set his gun on a table. From the expression on his face, she thought he was trying to figure out how to say something difficult. "We ... Belinda and I ... found Jimmy Hansik dead." With measured words, Abe provided the gloomy details, and his theory of what happened. The can of salmon had been eight months past the expiration date.

"My God," Peggy said as she sat on her bed, but she hardly had time to let the terrible news sink in. Looking down, she saw her baby's lips moving, making sucking motions. Peggy lifted her own gray fleece pullover so that Rosie could nurse, then felt the heartbreakingly weak suction of the child at her nipple.

In an emotionless voice, Abe looked away from the exposed breast and said, "We put his body in the cooling chamber with the others." It was as if he was making an announcement about the weather or the price of subzero parkas, as if he had no emotions left to grieve, or even be angry. But Peggy knew differently, and she couldn't fault him. Everyone in the seed repository had been through a great deal, and Abe had proven his courage and goodness to her.

"How's Belinda doing?" asked Peggy.

"Numb. I haven't seen her cry yet, but I'm sure at some point she will."

"I'll check in on her when I can," Peggy promised, though she didn't know where she was going to find the necessary energy. She felt a surge of guilt for even thinking that.

Cradling Rosie as the baby nursed, Peggy studied this rare man who had become her friend, noticing he had deteriorated to a shadow since she had met him, with flecks of gray hair at the temples and his hair increasingly disheveled. His brown eyes were so washed out and drained that they frightened her.

Abe came over, sat heavily next to her on the bed, and put an arm around her shoulders. They just sat there, saying nothing, as Rosie suckled at her mother's breast.

He was not there long when another uproar sounded outside, a tremendous crashing cacophony this time, and loud voices followed by gunfire. Startled, Peggy jerked back from her baby, but held onto her. Rosie screeched in protest, and continued to make sucking motions with her mouth.

Grabbing his handgun, Abe ran out into the corridor. The door slammed behind him.

Opening the door a little and peering down the corridor, Peggy saw Benitar Jackson and Abe Tojiko sheltered behind support columns, opening fire on the intruders as they streamed down the stairway with snow coming in all around them … men and women dressed in rags, their hair matted and straggly. Several bullets found their mark, and the wounded fell down the stairs, but others leaped around them, surging into the seed repository, followed by many more people, too numerous and hungry to care whether they exposed themselves to being shot or not. Some had their own guns, and fired back. Others carried knives and makeshift clubs.

Shot dead center in the chest, Benitar fell, shouting obscenities. He twitched, and went still.

"Food!" a man yelled in a deep voice. "They've got food down there!"

Terrified, Peggy saw Abe go into a crouching position, and then dash to another column. He glanced in her direction, a desperate, loving look.

A loud gunshot sounded. Abe crumpled to the floor, bleeding from the side of his head.

"No!" Peggy shouted.

With Rosie screaming and crying in her arms, Peggy saw the ragged intruders swarm into the corridor, and the snow blowing in from outside, around men and women looking like skeletons and yelling, "Food! Food!"

Unable to lock the door to her own room, Peggy saw the door to Benitar Jackson's room had been left open, something she'd never seen before. She ran with Rosie down the corridor and dashed into the Director's room, locking the door behind them. A small measure of security. Inside, she tried to soothe her crying baby, but Rosie was too agitated. She didn't even want to nurse.

Looking around the large sleeping quarters, Peggy saw another door open, an elevator. Having heard Abe's suspicions about what might be inside this room, she stepped inside. The door closed, and the elevator rose.

Stepping out into a chamber, she saw Benitar's white, bullet-shaped "seed-evacuation" capsule, unmistakable though she had never seen it before. This confirmed Abe's suspicions, but for some reason, perhaps because the Director didn't want to be slowed down if he needed to get away quickly, he had left everything open.

Downstairs, some of the intruders ran into the cooling chamber where the bodies were stored and food was kept. Belinda had followed them inside, in an attempt to save the seeds.

Watching the frenzied, starving men and women haul out the edibles, she moved to block their way, but it was like trying to stop a tidal wave. They yanked out and hauled away drawers and storage containers of seeds, tubers, bulbs and roots, as well as bodies and anything else that looked like food. To her dismay she saw a flurry of dirty hands around her, pushing her away, and the flashing glass of the containers. She heard the smashing and the breaking, mixed with the anguished cries of the mob as they cursed and fought over the limited supplies.

"Get away from it, you …"

"Mine! Mine! Mine!"

Inside the rooftop chamber, Peggy hurried into the escape capsule with her baby and sealed the cockpit. In her arms, Rosie had grown quiet, so she must have fallen asleep. Their body weight on the seat activated multi-colored lights around them. Studying the control panel and a simplified instruction panel next to it, Peggy figured out which buttons to press and which toggles to pull. On a red button, the words "Engine" and "PRESS" flashed alternately. With her free hand she did so, and heard the smooth whine of the capsule's engines, followed by the rough sound of the thick concrete rooftop hatch, as it opened to reveal a gray sky. Wind-blown snow flew in.

But the hatch stopped partway … jammed. Another damned electrical problem!

She pressed the button again, but nothing happened. Overhead, she saw people gathering around the outside of the rooftop hatch, looking down, with the whiteness of a storm swirling around them.

Helplessly, Peggy stared at a flashing blue button, the takeoff command, but she couldn't press it yet. Panicking, she tried the roof control again. More than anything, she needed to save her baby. Somewhere in the back of her mind she recalled hearing that the capsule also contained an assortment of seeds and other planting necessities, but they were of secondary importance to her. She could hardly think that far ahead.

After an excruciating delay, the rooftop hatch opened with a grinding noise, but stopped again before going all the way. She hammered on the button, but the hatch had gone as far as it would go. Was it enough?

She took a last look at Rosie, then took a chance for both of them. And with her palm, smacked the flashing blue takeoff button.

In the corridors on the main floor of the seed bank, Belinda saw people running in all directions, scooping up everything they could get their hands on, with snow blasting in from a blizzard, mixing with the seeds that scattered and disappeared into the whiteness.

To her surprise, she thought she understood a little how Benitar Jackson had felt. Maybe he had not been so crazy, after all.

In the midst of the commotion a fire began, burning through wood interior partitions, fixtures, and furnishings. The mob surged back up the stairs and out into the freezing whiteness.

With the bins emptied and smashed on the floor, and the last of the seeds scattered like snowflakes by the wind, Belinda felt the warmth of the fire. It had been a long time since she felt so warm. Despite everything, she found it pleasant.

Sitting down on the snowy stairs, she closed her eyes, feeling the warmth. It was nice. So nice. If nothing else, at least she was warm.

Like locusts, people began dropping through the rooftop opening, onto the deck all around the white capsule and on top of it. With feral, inquisitive eyes, they peered through the windshield and the top of the cockpit at Peggy and the baby she clutched so tightly.

Why isn't this thing taking off? she wondered in desperation, as the engines continued to whine, accelerating and decelerating. *Does it sense that the hatch isn't open far enough?*

Looking into her baby's face, Peggy saw the tiny blue eyes staring ahead, looking past her as if they were no longer capable of seeing anything. In an anguish unmatched in all of humanity, the young mother screamed. Then her precious child blinked, and cried. She was alive! The baby had her mother's fighting spirit.

You'll be all right, Rosie. Somehow we're going to make it.

As she pounded on the takeoff button, Peggy Atkins only half heard the people clamoring and trying to open compartments on the hull of the tiny vessel, intending to remove everything it contained, the food, the seeds, the emergency gear. Given the opportunity, they would rip off the cockpit cover and tear the wires out.

The lights on the control panel went dark, and she stopped pounding on it. Clutching Rosie to her, Peggy tried to preserve the warmth of her child's body, for as long as possible. She could do no more.

Alternate Ending

Then, when all seemed lost, the capsule suddenly surged upward and barely scraped past the opening in the rooftop hatch. In a matter of moments the vessel penetrated the dark cloud cover and escaped from the blizzard.

To her complete amazement Peggy beheld blue sky, like a gift from God, and she felt the glowing warmth of sunlight as it poured into the tiny cabin.

The capsule leveled out and flew smoothly over the cloud tops. Studying the instruments, she saw that the capsule was flying on its own, apparently on a pre-set, southeasterly course.

The desperate mother had no idea where she and Rosie would be taken, or if the destination ahead was even more abysmal than the place they had just left. Even so, she clung to a slender thread of hope. Maybe, against all odds, she could still find a way for them to survive.

About the Authors

Brian Herbert, the son of Frank Herbert, is the author of numerous *New York Times* bestsellers. He has won several literary honors and has been nominated for the highest awards in science fiction. In 2003, he published *Dreamer of Dune*, a moving biography of his father that was nominated for the Hugo Award. After writing ten *Dune*-universe novels with Kevin J. Anderson, the coauthors created their own epic series, *Hellhole*. In 2006, Brian began his own galaxy-spanning science fiction series with the novel *Timeweb*, followed by *The Web and the Stars* and *Webdancers*. His other acclaimed solo novels include *Sidney's Comet; Sudanna, Sudanna; The Race for God;* and *Man of Two Worlds* (written with Frank Herbert).

Website: dunenovels.com

Bruce Taylor, also known as "Mr. Magic Realism," writes magic realism and surrealism, as well as spiritual works. He is the author of *The Final Trick of Funnyman and Other Stories, Edward: Dancing on the Edge of Infinity, Mr. Magic Realism,* and *Mountains of the Night*. His book *Kafka's Uncle and other Strange Tales* was nominated for the &Now Award for Innovative Writing.

Bruce has been writer in residence at Shakespeare & Company, Paris, president of the Seattle Writers Association, president of the Seattle Freelances and co-director of The Wellness Program at Harborview Medical Center.

A hypnotherapist and avid backpacker, Bruce teaches fiction writing for the ArtsNow Program at Edmonds Community College near Seattle. He lives in Seattle with his partner, Roberta Gregory, and their fickle feline, Purrrzac.

Website: BruceBTaylor.com